Lucy's Feet

by
Stephanie Stein

Perspectives Press
P.O. Box 90318
Indianapolis, IN 46290-0318

Illustrated by Kathryn A. Imler

> Perspectives Press
> P.O. Box 90318
> Indianapolis, IN 46290-0318

Manufactured in Mexico on acid-free paper.
ISBN 0-944934-05-6

Library of Congress Cataloging in Publication Data

Stein, Stephanie, 1953-
    Lucy's feet/by Stephanie Stein: [Kathryn A. Imler, illustrator].
    p.   cm.
    Summary: Eight-year-old Lucy is suddenly hit uncomfortably with the meaning of her having been adopted by her parents, while her new baby brother was born to them.
    ISBN 0-944934-05-6: $12.95
    [1. Adoption—Fiction.] I. Imler, Kathryn A., 1950-   ill.
II. Title.
PZ7.S82164Lu 1992
[E]—dc20

                        92-4602
                          CIP
                          AC

Other books from Perspectives Press, the Infertility and Adoption Publisher

The Mulberry Bird: Story of an Adoption	Our Baby: A Birth and Adoption Story
Real for Sure Sister	Where the Sun Kisses the Sea
Filling in the Blanks: A Guided Look at Growing Up Adopted	William Is My Brother
	And other <u>adult</u> books

Write the publisher for a detailed catalog and ordering information.

Dedications

From the Author
This book is dedicated to the memory of my mother, Gloria Stein,
who taught me a great many things. And to Emma, who continues to
teach me.

Stephanie Stein

From the Illustrator
For my mother and father, and for John, Anne, Margaret, Mary Beth,
Julie, and Joanie.

Kathryn A. Imler

Lucy liked her feet. They were sturdy and strong, and most of the time they stood firm upon the ground. Sometimes, when Lucy thought no one was looking, she poked about between her toes, searching carefully, until she found some lint.

As far as Lucy was concerned, any kind of lint would do: sock lint, carpet lint, any kind of fluff or stuff that would settle down between her toes. Sometimes sand, or funny things like pieces of crackers and even cheese would find their way between Lucy's toes! But Lucy, who was getting more grown up each day, knew the difference between lint and crackers and cheese.

She poked about between her toes, searching carefully, until she found some lint.

"Wherever did she get such a strange habit?" asked Lucy's mother, whenever Lucy pulled off her shoes and socks and began her hunt for lint.

Lucy's dad would wink at Lucy, shrug his shoulders halfway to the sky, and say, "Why, I just can't imagine!"

Then, while Lucy and her father giggled, they would look straight at Lucy's mom. Because, without a doubt, that's exactly where Lucy learned to search between her toes for whatever might be caught there. When Lucy's mom thought no one was looking, she poked about between her toes, looking for lint. And whenever Lucy asked her what she was doing, she always said, "Nothing, dear. Just trimming my cuticles."

Lucy didn't understand what cuticles were, but she did know all about searching for lint— especially the kind that liked to hide between her toes.

"Why, I just can't imagine!"

Lucy liked her feet when they carried her
dizzily across the room, as she leapt and
pirouetted at dancing school. At times like
this Lucy felt that she could fly.

She leapt and pirouetted at dancing school.

She ran and kicked, fast and hard.

Lucy liked her feet at soccer games, when she ran and kicked, fast and hard. She would always get breathless, and her heart would beat fast within her chest. At times like this Lucy was filled with pride. People would shout, "Go, Lucy, go!" and sometimes, but not all the time, Lucy's feet would carry her to victory.

Perhaps best of all, Lucy liked her feet when her silly Aunt Ollie, whose toes were always painted bright red, came to visit. Aunt Ollie would take out her nail polish and paint Lucy's toenails fire-engine red. Lucy liked to put all of her ten red toes right next to Aunt Ollie's ten red toes. And then she would say, "See, Aunt Ollie, we look exactly alike!" Then Aunt Ollie would swoop Lucy up in her arms and kiss her and hug her, and sometimes, but not all the time, she would kiss all ten of Lucy's lovely red toes.

Lucy liked to put all of her ten red toes right next to Aunt Ollie's ten red toes.

Lucy's feet could get her into trouble, too. Theodore, at dancing school, always teased Lucy about her wild red hair and her long, skinny feet. Sometimes, when no one was looking, he'd stick his tongue out right in front of Lucy's face.

One day, Theodore said to Lucy, "I know why you have red hair and your mother has black hair and your father has black hair and your baby brother Elliott has black hair. My mom told me. You're adopted!"

Lucy tried not to listen to Theodore. She spun round and round, faster and faster. Theodore went on, "Adopted means you didn't grow inside your mother the way Elliott did."

"I know why you have red hair."

Lucy stopped spinning and said, "Red hair runs in the family. On both sides."

But before you could say "pirouette," Lucy, who had been pointing and flexing those lovely and strong ballerina feet, kicked Theodore—accidentally of course—right in the seat of his pants.

Then Theodore was crying, and Lucy was crying, and poor Miss Paulina looked like she might cry, too. But Miss Paulina didn't cry. She yelled. And on that troubled day it seemed as if she didn't stop yelling until it was time to go home. At home, Lucy's mom yelled some more, as if Lucy hadn't heard enough about what she had done wrong. And Lucy blamed it all on her strong, willful, ballerina-twirling, soccer-kicking feet.

Then she pressed her bare toes right up against her aunt's nose.

Today the sun sparkled high up in the sky, and Lucy's Aunt Ollie had come to visit. After Aunt Ollie kissed Lucy about a million times, and after she threw Lucy's baby brother Elliott up in the air about a million times, she sat down on the sofa to talk and talk and talk to Lucy's mom.

Then Aunt Ollie, who was always very silly, began to kiss Lucy's feet. Lucy laughed and tried to wriggle free. Then she pressed her bare toes right up against her aunt's nose. Aunt Ollie made a funny face and began to moan and groan.

"What smelly toes you have!" she said.

And, Lucy, who always liked this game, shouted, "My feet don't smell!"

"Ollie," Lucy's mom said. "What are you doing to my child?"

"I'm polishing her toes." And Aunt Ollie took out her red nail polish from her big, fat bag, and she began to polish Lucy's toenails fire-engine red.

The hardest part about toenail polish is not touching those toes until they're dry. So Lucy sat and sat, and she admired her feet. She couldn't help but poke a little at those feet, but she tried not to touch those very shiny toes.

All of a sudden she heard Aunt Ollie say to her mother, "Why this child has your feet! Look. Each toe could be yours."

Lucy looked.

Aunt Ollie wasn't talking about Lucy's feet, which looked absolutely stunning with those bright red toes. She was talking about Elliott's feet. In fact, at that very moment, one of Elliott's feet was being waved about in the air by Aunt Ollie. Elliot, who sat in his aunt's lap, began to giggle. (What a dumb giggle, Lucy thought.)

Lucy's mom looked too. "What are you talking about?" she said.

"Your son's feet. Look. They're exactly like yours," Aunt Ollie said.

Just then Lucy, who had been practicing her arabesque, watched in surprise as her foot lurched out and caught Aunt Ollie by the seat of her pants.

"Lucy! You kicked me," Aunt Ollie said. She looked surprised.

"I was just practicing my arabesque, and you got in the way!" Lucy tried to explain. Aunt Ollie and Mommy looked upset.

"Well, make sure you don't do that again. You might hurt someone." Aunt Ollie was not being silly now.

"Apologize to your aunt," said Lucy's mom. This, too, was not pretend.

"Lucy! You kicked me."

"But whose feet do I have?" Lucy asked.

"You have your feet," said Aunt Ollie.
"You have my feet, too." And she wiggled
her feet out of her shoes and planted all ten
of her red toes right next to Lucy's ten red
toes.

Lucy was confused. Lucy was mad, too.

"This is a weird family," Lucy said.

"You have a point there," Lucy's mom said.
"Your aunt kisses your toes. That's pretty
weird."

"And you pick lint out of your toes when
no one is looking!" shouted Lucy.

"You have a point there, too," said Lucy's
mom.

Aunt Ollie planted all ten of her red toes right next to Lucy's ten red toes.

"But that's not what I mean," Lucy said. Lucy was feeling sad.

"I don't want to be adopted! It's not fair. Elliott has your feet because he grew inside there," said Lucy, pointing to her mother's stomach. "It's not fair! How come I was adopted and he wasn't? I want to come from in there, too!"

"I want to come from in there, too!"

For a moment, everyone in the house was still. Even Elliott.

Lucy's mother pulled her daughter close and hugged her tightly. "I wish you grew in there, too," she said.

Lucy struggled free from her mom. Elliott began to fidget and Aunt Ollie picked him up.

"You know, Lucy, in a way you did grow in here," said Lucy's mom.

Lucy looked up. She had been looking down at her feet. "What do you mean?" she said.

Lucy's mother pulled her daughter close and hugged her tightly.

"She's kicking away at my heart."

"Elliott grew inside my body, but my love for you, my wanting you, grew in here." Lucy's mom pointed to her heart.

"But you couldn't feel me in there, the way you could when Elliott kicked before he was born."

"Oh yes I could!" said Lucy's mom. "I carried you around in my heart for a very long time. And while I waited I thought about the little baby that would be mine someday. I thought about what you would look like. I thought about how it would feel when I held you close. I thought about the songs we would sing and the places we would go. Then my heart would start beating very fast, and I would think 'Now that's my baby kicking, only she's not kicking at my stomach, she's kicking away at my heart.'"

Lucy let out a long, deep breath.

I want to practice my arabesque!" said Lucy, who was getting tired from all this talk. But tired or not, Lucy felt like she could fly.

Lucy pointed her lovely toes and began to swirl around the room. She swirled past her mom. She swirled past her silly Aunt Ollie. Lucy swirled past her baby brother Elliott. As Lucy leapt and pirouetted around the room, she noticed that her smart baby brother was poking about between his toes, and she giggled.

She knew that he was looking for lint.